T0198823

The Tale

of

Chicken Noodle

and

Rabbit Stew Number Two

Written by Arlene Gerrity

Illustrated by J.J. Walsh

Order this book online at www.trafford.com
or email orders@trafford.com

Most Trafford titles are also available at major online book retailers.

 www.trafford.com

North America & international
toll-free: 844 688 6899 (USA & Canada)
fax: 812 355 4082

Our mission is to efficiently provide the world's finest, most comprehensive book publishing service, enabling every author to experience success. To find out how to publish your book, your way, and have it available worldwide, visit us online at www.trafford.com

Because of the dynamic nature of the Internet, any web addresses or links contained in this book may have changed since publication and may no longer be valid. The views expressed in this work are solely those of the author and do not necessarily reflect the views of the publisher, and the publisher hereby disclaims any responsibility for them.

Any people depicted in stock imagery provided by Getty Images are models, and such images are being used for illustrative purposes only. Certain stock imagery © Getty Images.

ISBN: 978-1-4251-6258-0

Print information available on the last page.

Trafford rev. 02/27/2023

Once there was a little chicken, and his name was Chicken Noodle. He loved strawberry milk, vegetable soup and delicious apple strudel.

Every morning his mother would say "Wake up my little noodle. It's time to get ready for school, so don't you diddly doodle."

Little noodle always did what his mother said. He ate his breakfast, brushed his beak, and then he made his bed.

Chicken Noodle had three friends, Doggie Biscuit, and Horsey Shoe. But his very best friend in the whole world was Rabbit Stew Number Two.

When Chicken went to school one day, he got a sad surprise. Rabbit's chair was empty, and he couldn't believe his eyes.

After school, all three friends asked
everyone they knew,

"Have you seen our dear, dear friend,
Rabbit Stew Number Two?"

Rabbit Stew Number One was in the playpen sucking his thumb.

Rabbit Stew Number Three was in the kitchen making tea.

Rabbit Stew Number Four,

STORE

CARROTS
4
SALE

Was with his grandma at the grocery store.

Rabbit Stew Number Five was in the pool taking a dive.

Rabbit Stew Number Six was teaching his puppy some brand new tricks.

Rabbit Stew Number Seven was reading a book about angels and heaven.

Rabbit Stew Number Eight was eating
a piece of birthday cake.

Rabbit Stew Number Nine was hanging his laundry on the clothes line.

Rabbit Stew Number Ten was helping them look for Rabbit, but then!

Mother Rabbit was walking her poodle and stopped to talk to Chicken Noodle.

"Please don't worry, please don't fret.
Don't get yourself all upset.
Nothing has happened to Number Two.
He's only in bed getting over the flu."

Now all four friends were together
again, friends so brave and true.
Laughing, talking and just being
happy with Rabbit Stew Number Two.

Printed in the United States
by Baker & Taylor Publisher Services